The Selkie Child

Story retold by Gill Howell
Pictures by Sophie Keen

...dingles&company...

The legend

There is a story that is told by the people who live on the rocky shores of the northern islands. Some believe it is true; some say that it is just a legend. It tells of the seal people, called Selkies. The Selkies leave the sea to become human for one night and one day. They hide their sealskins among the rocks, for they must find them again in order to return to the waves.

Some say it happens every nine tides and some that it occurs on Midsummer's Eve. Some say that a Selkie can be called onto the shore if you weep seven tears into the sea. All agree that Selkies have a haunting beauty.

John Wilson and his wife, Kate, lived a contented life in their little house facing the sea. The house crouched against the cliffs, lashed by winter storms and baked by summer suns. John loved the sea and went each day to chase the shoals of fish off the shore in his fishing boat.

4

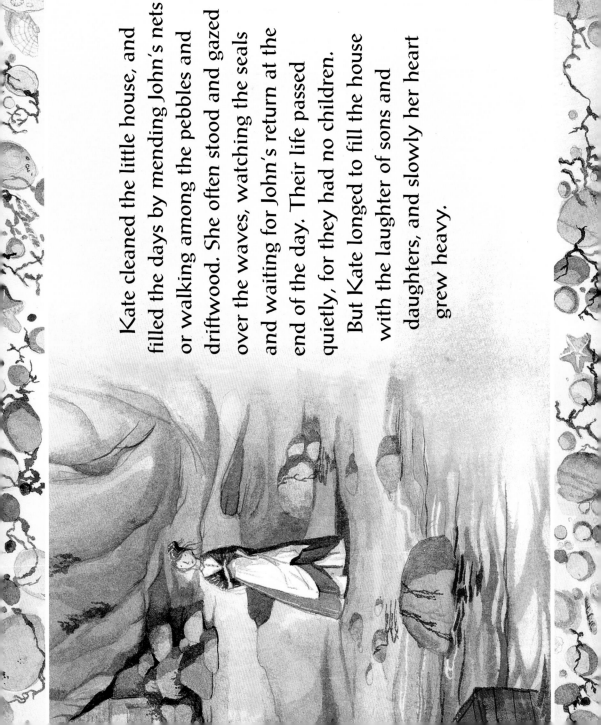

Kate cleaned the little house, and filled the days by mending John's nets or walking among the pebbles and driftwood. She often stood and gazed over the waves, watching the seals and waiting for John's return at the end of the day. Their life passed quietly, for they had no children. But Kate longed to fill the house with the laughter of sons and daughters, and slowly her heart grew heavy.

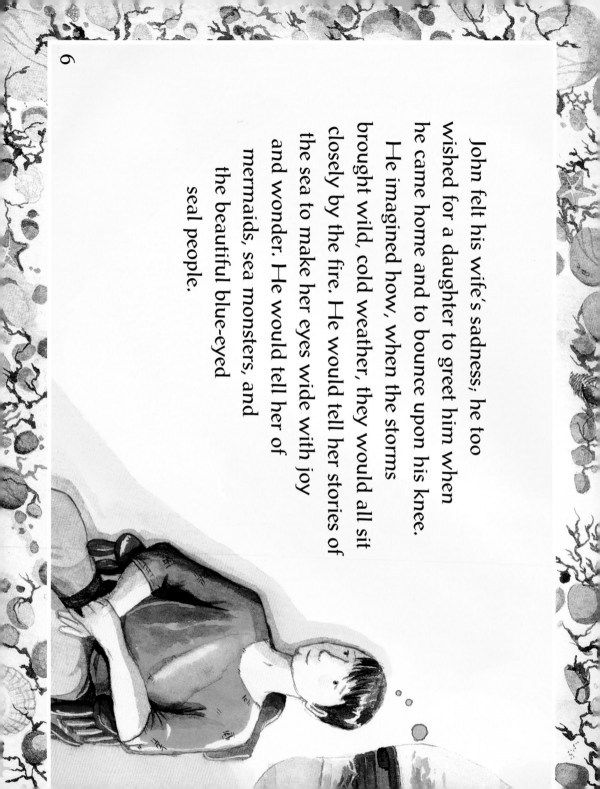

John felt his wife's sadness; he too wished for a daughter to greet him when he came home and to bounce upon his knee.

He imagined how, when the storms brought wild, cold weather, they would all sit closely by the fire. He would tell her stories of the sea to make her eyes wide with joy and wonder. He would tell her of mermaids, sea monsters, and the beautiful blue-eyed seal people.

When the sun shone and warm winds came, he would take his daughter along the shore. They would find driftwood, pebbles, and treasure from the sea. He would teach her to swim like a seal, and take her out fishing in his boat.

But as time passed, their home stayed childless.

One winter night a great
storm blew up. The sea
swirled in a fury. Strong
winds lashed the water. The
waves crashed upon the
shore. Kate feared they
would wash up to the
very walls of the
little house.

When morning came and the wind had died away, John went out to see what the storm had brought. The cries of gray and white gulls filled the air above the cliffs, blown inland by the gale. Now the sea was calm again, and John gazed along the rocky beach over the glistening gray rocks and pebbles that lined the shore. Driftwood, bleached by the salt, was turned to silver in the watery sunlight.

But there, where the pebbles met the waves, John saw something moving. As he drew closer, he found a small child, lying on a bed of seaweed.

"Here is a strange gift from the sea!" cried John. As he stared in wonder, he saw a glossy brown skin nearby in a crack in the rocks. Quickly he bent, snatched it up, and hid it in his pocket.

John went to pick up the child and he wrapped her inside his warm coat. As the child looked up at John, she seemed to hold all the mysteries of the sea in her clear, crystal-blue eyes.

"Kate! Kate!" called John as he made his way back to the little house. "See what the storm has left us – a deserted child alone among the rocks!"

John and Kate took the child in and named her Morgan, meaning "born of the sea".

John locked the skin away in a big chest, tucked it into a dark corner, and said nothing about it to Kate.

They both talked and laughed happily with the child each evening and gazed with love into her pale, crystal-blue eyes. But though Morgan's laughter filled the house with joy, no other sound passed her lips.

Nobody came to claim the child, nor was any search heard of. So John and Kate kept her as their own daughter and were happy.

John sang as he took his boat out fishing each day, and Kate sang as she rocked Morgan on her lap.

As the days passed, Morgan seemed content. Kate cared for her lovingly and she grew plump and rosy-cheeked. John told her stories of the sea, of storms and great waves that swamped the boats, of monsters and mermaids, and of the legend of the beautiful seal people.

Slowly, as the days turned into
weeks, Morgan's blue eyes bent
more and more toward the sea.
They seemed full of longing,
and Kate felt her sorrow.
Laughter and song left
the little house by the sea.
In the evenings, as the sun
was sinking, the harsh
cries of the gulls joined
the calls of the seals
along the shoreline.
Kate's heart grew
heavy once more.

One day, while Morgan
slept, Kate walked with John
along the shore. The seals
seemed to be watching them.
For a time they both stood
silently, gazing out to sea. Then
Kate bent to touch the place
where Morgan had been
found among the pebbles.

"John, I fear that Morgan is no mortal child," she told him. "What else did you see on the shore when you found her?"

"There was nothing – only the child," he replied, and left quickly to go fishing.

As the days lengthened into spring, Kate busied herself with chores. Morgan grew listless and pale. Only when she heard the calls of the seals did Morgan's fading blue eyes grow crystal-bright again.

One morning, while John was away at sea, the sunlight shone into the house and its beams caught an old dusty chest tucked away in a corner.

"What old treasures have we kept in here?" wondered Kate.

She was puzzled when she found it locked. So, taking up a strong knife, Kate pried it open and was amazed to hear Morgan's laughter bubbling up with delight behind her.

There, at the
bottom of the chest,
tucked underneath
old blankets and
worn shoes, was a
glossy sealskin.
Kate then knew
that what she
had feared was
true. Morgan
was a Selkie
child.

At once she gathered up the child in her arms, and taking the sealskin with her, quickly picked her way through the rocks and driftwood down to the sea. The seals had gathered off the shore, floating silently in the swell of the waves, watching. Kate kissed the child fondly, as she wrapped her in the skin. Then, without a pause, she gently placed Morgan into the shallows.

Kate stayed on the shore as the sun moved across the sky. She saw Morgan swim away without a backward glance. She watched the seals greet the Selkie child and thought she saw them swirling and turning in the sea as if rejoicing in the child's return. In her grief, seven teardrops fell from her eyes and splashed into the water. Then she turned for home.

The Selkie King watched Kate and saw her kindness. He was Morgan's true father and understood the sorrow of losing a child.

"Seven tears for seven children," he said.

As the years went by, Kate and John's house became full of the laughter of children as their family grew. Four sons and three daughters brought joy to the little house on the shore by the sea. And through the kindness of the Selkie King they lived in happiness all the rest of their days.